KETCHUP

How to
Raise a Mom

by Jean Reagan   illustrated by Lee Wildish

ALFRED A. KNOPF   NEW YORK

For moms all
around the world,
but especially mine!
–J.R.

Thanks, Mum.
–L.W.

THIS IS A BORZOI BOOK PUBLISHED BY ALFRED A. KNOPF

Text copyright © 2017 by Jean Reagan
Jacket art and interior illustrations copyright © 2017 by Lee Wildish

All rights reserved. Published in the United States by Alfred A. Knopf, an imprint of Random House Children's Books,
a division of Penguin Random House LLC, New York.

Visit us on the Web! randomhousekids.com

Educators and librarians, for a variety of teaching tools, visit us at RHTeachersLibrarians.com

Library of Congress Cataloging-in-Publication Data
Reagan, Jean.
How to raise a mom / by Jean Reagan ; illustrated by Lee Wildish. — First edition.
pages cm.
Summary: Provides instructions for raising a happy,
healthy mother, including introducing such stress-reducing activities as
searching for wiggly worms, painting rainbows, eating snacks, and playing
with toys.
ISBN 978-0-553-53829-8 (hardcover) — ISBN 978-0-553-53830-4 (lib. bdg.) — ISBN 978-0-553-53831-1 (ebook)
I. Mothers—Fiction.
PZ7.R2354 Hqp 20172014
[E]—dc23
2015040178

The text of this book is set in 18-point Goudy Old Style.
The illustrations were created digitally.
MANUFACTURED IN CHINA
March 2017
10 9 8 7 6 5 4 3 2

First Edition

Raising a happy, healthy mom is fun . . . *and* important!
Are you ready for some tips?

First of all, help your mom ease into the day.

HOW TO START HER MORNING:

- Let her sleep in, just a little longer.

- Then kiss, kiss, kiss her awake.

- Fling open the curtains and say, "Rise and shine! Your breakfast is ready."

When it's time to get dressed, be sure to give her choices.

HOW TO DRESS A MOM:

Not too serious.

Not too silly.

Not too sparkly.

Perfect!

A mom can forget things when she's hurrying to leave the house.
So help her by piling it all at the door:

snacks, toys, purse, keys, phone,
shopping list, library books to return,
letters to mail, more snacks and more toys.

Errands are fun, until . . .
you end up in a looooooooong line.

If your mom starts to
get a little cranky . . .

Surprise her with
a snack and toy.

If that doesn't work . . .
act out a goofy story.

If that *still* doesn't work, try saying,
in a very cheerful voice, "Thank you so
much, Sweet Pea, for being *so* patient."

When you're *finally* done, if you're lucky—you might run into a friend. Right away, plan a playdate for your mom.

Whisper: "Remember to be a good sharer!"

Back at home, if your mom has work to do, tell her, "It's quiet time. *Shhhhhh.*"

Then start your own project.

On regular days—you've probably noticed—
moms tidy up, without being asked.
Today, it's your turn!

A happy, healthy, STRONG mom needs . . . exercise!

HOW TO EXERCISE WITH A MOM:

Take turns scoring goals.

Race against the wind.

Hop like a kangaroo.

Swing like a monkey.

Slither like a snake.

When your mom's all tired out, show her the best ways to relax.

HOW TO RELAX:

- Hold a yoga pose for as long as you can.

- Lie in the grass and look for wiggly worms, slimy snails, and roly-poly bugs.

- Sing her a lullaby.

Rock-a-bye, Mommy,
sleeping under the tree . . .

But what if rainy weather keeps you stuck inside?

HOW TO ENTERTAIN A MOM INSIDE:

Plan an indoor beach day.

Teach her how to
paint rainbows.

Set up a zoo all across the floor.
(Don't forget the sharks!)

Soon it's time for dinner, and that most surely means . . . vegetables.
If your mom's a picky eater, **try these tricks:**

- Broccoli – Pretend she's a dinosaur gobbling
  up the trees. *Roar, chomp, chew!*

- Cauliflower – They're snowy-day trees.
  ROAR, CHOMP, CHEW!

- Carrots – Make them into a heart.

- Give her a choice: "Which will you
  eat first–your peas or your beans?"

When it starts to get dark, your mom may want to skip right to bedtime stories. But tell her, "Nope, not yet.

First you have to:
put-away-your-toys-
wash-your-face-
put-on-your-pajamas-
brush-your-teeth-
hop-into-bed."

Now it's time for stories.
If she asks, "One more, please?" Say, "Okay." But just once.
Remind her it's important to get to sleep on time.

Then snuggle up and ask, "What was the best thing about today?"

She'll snuggle back and say, "You!"

. . . and *that's* how you raise a happy, healthy mom.